I0727213

MORNINGSTAR

Book One- The Mystery of the Secret Book

MORNINGSTAR

Book One- The Mystery of the Secret Book

ONDI LAURE

Morningstar; Book One- The Mystery of the Secret Book
Copyright © 2024 Ondi Laure
All rights reserved.

No part of this book may be reproduced, stored in a retrieval system, or transmitted in any form or by any means—electronic, mechanical, photocopying, recording, or otherwise—without the prior written permission of the copyright holder. The only exception is by a reviewer, who may quote short excerpts in a review with appropriate citations.

Book cover design by Debbie O'Byrne www.jetlaunch.net
Book interior design by www.digitalcc.us
Editing by Rhonda Cawthorn

Follow the author:
website: www.OndiLaure.com
LinkedIn: www.linkedin.com/in/OlShepp
Twitter: www.twitter.com/OLShepp
Instagram: www.instagram.com/OndiLaure/
Facebook: www.facebook.com/OLShepp
Resources & Communities Linktr.ee: www.MyInkLinks.com

Published by Story Launcher LLC: http://storylauncher.com

ISBN-13: 978-1-951451-17-2 (KINDLE)
ISBN-13: 978-1-951451-16-5 (PAPER BACK)
ISBN-13; 978-1-951451-03-5 (Audio)

Scriptures taken from The Gnostic Society Library © 1995-2005 Lance Owens and The Bible Manuscript Society © 2013-2019 Used by permission. All rights reserved.

Disclaimer: Morningstar is a work of historical fiction. All names and characters are either invented or used fictitious. Any resemblance to actual persons is coincidental. To the best of the author's experience (her brush with death and her visit to an alternate dimension), heaven and our earthly realm are close. Moreover, while many events described in this book are historically accurate, God's boundless totality of being feminine, Sophia as much as being masculine, Jesus has yet to be authentically represented in historical scripture.

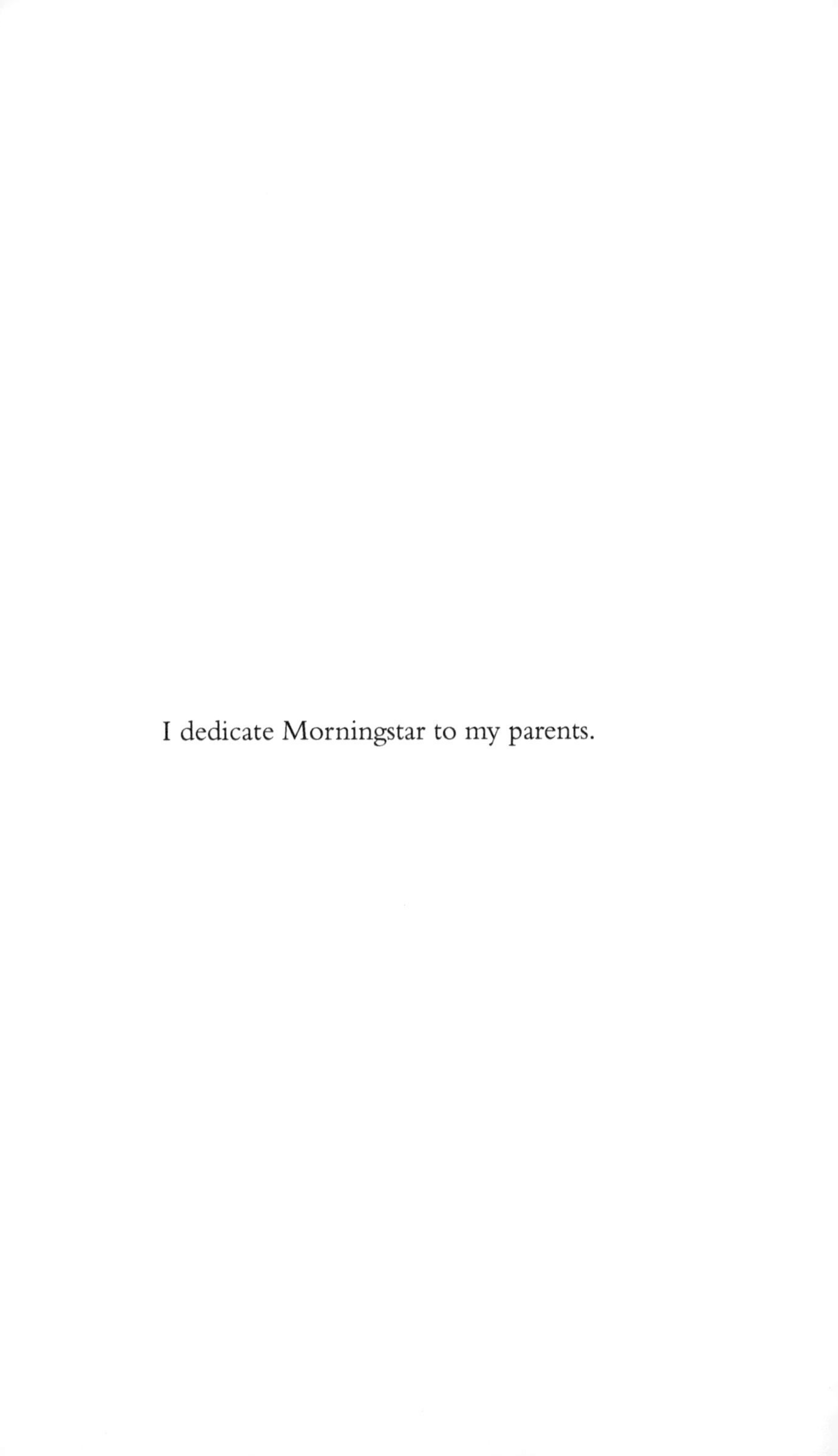

I dedicate Morningstar to my parents.

*"Beware that no one lead you astray saying Lo
here or lo there! For the Son of Man is within you.
Follow after Him!"*

The Gospel Of Mary 4: 34-35

Table of Contents

Acknowledgments

I thank my mother for her continued support, feedback, and ongoing critiquing of Morningstar. It would not have become a finished novel without her faith in me.

I thank my dad for his inspiration for the character Charles, an artist trapped in a war zone. Though his story took place centuries later in Vietnam, the theme remains.

Preface

"The plan of the universe. Is not that which
we all seek? And did not Jesus himself explain that their
speculations have not reached the truth?[3] I recall Joseph's
interpretation he read upon the Al-Aora that Providence
has no wisdom in it. And fate does not discern. But to you
it is given to know; and whoever is worthy
of knowledge will receive it."[20]

Morningstar, Book One (11: 81-82)

The Gospel of Mary – although we only have tatters of the original manuscript, discovered in 1896, some 80 years before the discovery of the Dead Sea Scrolls and labeled "gnostic ." Even in the Gospel of Mary (Magdalene), though Jesus names her his favorite Disciple—one whom even the other disciples acknowledge, is beloved more than all the other disciples and is so beloved by the Savior that he kisses her full on the mouth—she is almost silenced by disciples like Peter who are jealous that the Savior made his final appearance to her in his spirit. Mary Magdalene was not only Jesus' most beloved Disciple but also one who was given a position of great honor and divine leadership. She was appointed to speak her vision and prophecy to the jealous disciples and motivate them to go about their business and spread The Word. Mary is praised by the Savior because she has not 'wavered' at the sight of him. The Savior ascribes Mary's stability to the fact that her mind is concentrated on spiritual matters. Mary clearly attained the purity of mind necessary to see and converse with the Savior.

Throughout history, women have been silenced—from the beginnings of known humanity. Preachers and prophets such as Saint Philomena were beheaded for refusing to sacrifice a life or sworn chastity for an evil emperor's hand in marriage (3rd cen. A.D.) to Perpetua and Felicitas, who spoke out about their right to practice their Christian faith and were tortured by wild animals in an arena and eventually, the sword. From the more famed Joan of Arc, who was famously vocal in her prophecies until she was burned at the stake, to more recently, Malala Yousafzai, a Pakistani student shot in the head and silenced by Taliban terrorists, for speaking out about the rights of women everywhere to get an education, even in the Middle East. Women have been silenced by men seeking to wipe out not just their voice but their divine nature, their intuition, their power, from written scouts, oral accounts, from history.

"The Good" restores us back to our source and
our "Good" within. The Gospel of Mary 4:27

I invite you to walk with me as Saren's story unravels
the secrets lost in the pages of The Gospel of Mary. Mary
Magdalene's story and the lessons taught her as Saren
embarks upon her divinely inspired journey of uncovering,
protecting, and learning forgotten truths and insights of the
human experience. Join to re-actualize women's position in
scripture, history, and in our historical and cultural moment
then and now; I tell a story of the erasure of women from
Mary to Saren and let their voices join in song.

BOOK I

CHAPTER ONE

The Brittling Of The Deer

Saren needed her mom. She wanted her mom as the waves want the moon. *What am I to do without a mother?* She thought as she squeezed her eyes closed, pushing the worrisome thought aside, and instead chose to remember the silly talks they would have about fathers, husbands, suitors, and babies. The many talks about the babies that her mom could not carry long enough to be born alive. Again, Saren pushed her sadness aside with happy memories of sewing and mending dresses, laughing about men, feeding their bodies, and fueling their souls.

The quiet breeze from the Frisian Sea on early spring mornings blows shivers upon Saren's skin. Shivers that linger and, like her dreams, are filled with ghosts. Ghosts who try to comfort her with their cold spirit hands, but she can never see their faces. They are like smoke, like steam, like the clouds that sometimes appear in the night sky among the stars.

She chases these ghosts, trembling from desperation and crying in her sleep. Calling for the ghost, she wants to see so much that she wakes tired, and her bones are like lead.

Saren believes sometimes that her mother would manifest from her yearning alone. Perhaps standing behind her when she looks at her reflection in the water.

Couldn't she feel her sorrow from wherever the dead go?

Wishing with all her heart, *she could see her mother, even when awake, because she wanted to. She needed to.* "Perhaps her spirit lingers," Saren prayed. "So, I don't die from grief?

Sound became Saren's refuge—it dispelled all thoughts about ghosts, heartache, and her mother. Sound. *That's it*, Saren thought, *that will take it all away . . .* constant, unceasing sound . . .

Anything but her thoughts, or dreams, or the sound of the beautiful, crystal, indifferent sea. Its wistful and yearning waves made her miss her mother even more. The sea was the color of her mom's eyes, blue and clear as glass.

Before the deep sadness could hit, she fled toward the comfort of her father, her Nan, and their music. She knew that her father would try to eat heartily so that she would also, but Saren instead tapped her spoon and fidgeted, leaving no time for eating.

Her father's bagpipes filled the air with happier music. Vibrations that touched each fiber of her soul and numbed the hurt. Even if it was only momentary, they were beautiful and welcome moments when the Heavy weight vanished. However, as Saren was learning, they always returned.

Lately, Father played battle hymns in the mornings while trudging in the wet, dawn sand. These songs spoke of bravery and being stalwart in strife, even for a now-motherless young woman.

No wonder she was sensing his departure, Saren thought before she knew it. *Of course.* Three battle hymns were her warning and his farewell. His way to prepare her for his now-obvious departure.

Often around dusk, she'd find him staring at the sea, his brow knit with worry.

It was becoming clear to her little by little, like the chickens she tried to chase in the early morning fog. Eventually, the mist fades, and you can see their feathered backs. And catch them.

Perhaps, she thought, his bagpipes don't dispel his pain as it does mine, Saren thought, *but across that water was work, war, and the distractions of something BIG to do for King Richard that just might be able to.*

CHAPTER TWO

This New Kind Of War

Her father's, Charles's, grief was becoming clear to Saren's adolescent reasoning as she knew him to play his orphic and torturous tributes for her mother up and down the beach. His aloneness there upon the shore of the Frisian Sea roared. His grief had become different. It had taken on a new source, a tension, like a knot that was tied too tight and about to unravel. This feeling must be like relief and much more manageable than sorrow. Her father had grown fidgety and restless. He moved antically as if trying to run from something and trying to send his orphic hymns to her mother to coax her home. Although often plaintive, his playing helped Saren with her pain, even if it couldn't quiet his own, as he seemed to know.

Saren realized now a feeling her father needed badly—a feeling to run toward—a feeling that lured him with sounds of swords clashing, the fury of men, and the noble, astounding pride of winning a battle. And she knew, most certainly, that he couldn't wait for this *new* kind of war.

Saren would wake to her father's celebratory tribute to his Mina as if he could compel her to return to them with the force of the emotions he blew upon the reeds.

Yes, it was her religion, which did not pertain to any deity or fable the Crown encouraged. Her religion was the love she witnessed in her father there upon the shore as he played his bagpipes, his breast heaving. His faith in his ability to entertain her mother across the reaches of the universe, proved to Saren that love, at least, is eternal.

"Do you fancy she can hear you?" Saren called one morning as he played until he was red-cheeked and winded. To sweeten her words, she approached him, reaching across the wind. "Do you think she'll return the more you play or the louder you play?"

"Knowing she hears me play is enough," he called back.

"You say that as if you are so certain," Saren mumbled quietly.

Her father turned to look into her eyes. "I *am* certain."

"Come, my Saren, let us go to the house for our lessons await us. They won't practice themselves, now. Will they?"

With their hands clasped and his pipes loosely slung upon his shoulder, they leaped from one stone to another across the stony trail to the brothy at Alnwick. Closing the seaward sky behind them as night surrendered to the amber light.

The kitchen fire smoldered warm beneath Nan's heavy caldron, the cauldron she used for every meal and potion. Her Nan stooped nearer the fire, her smile reappeared, and her eyes glistened as tears fell from her lashes into the morning pottage.

Saren retrieved her kerchief. As she set a peat brick into the coals, she left it in Nan's hand with a wink and a quick peck on her cheek.

"Thank ye, thank ye," Nan straightened her spine the best she could and gathered her family around the morning table. "Thank all the stars of the night's sky for our hefty pottage. Saren, a blessing from ye?" she directed.

"Thank all the stars of the morning's sky and for your hearty pottage, dear Nan, for what ought the pair of us do without your hearty potions to fuel our bellies?" Charles interjected as he squeezed his mother-in-law's weathered hand.

Saren's days were changing. She almost missed the ghosts that followed her dreams into the light. Now her dreams were filled with a sense of bittersweet farewell. Her mother, she figured, encouraging her to keep going with all routine abandoned here for each of the three of them.

With the morning meal over, Saren cleared the dishes and spread a map across the birch table, trying to tame down its scrolled ends. The old map was withering and becoming almost transparent.

"Can you even see the path?" Saren asked her father.

In the faint light from the fire and a lonely candle's flicker, memory was Charles's guide. He spoke of the vast regions to the north, his forefathers' homelands past Northumberland. Generations had fought over the pebbly shores long before he was born, and they would continue to fight.

He laughed, "Your children's children may fight for this same heap of rocks, this cladach, as I. Aye, Lass. It is our home and worth fighting for."

They studied the map to determine their approaching journey. Their mission to share the word of God written in English, Gaelic, or Celtic.

Her father schooled her widely, with daily lessons of knighthood, English, and histories of the Scots. Latin speaking and reading, writing, mathematics, and most important of all, according to Father, *survival*.

"Here is where you must go if conflict or war arises." Charles pressed his thumb atop London on the soiled map. He rubbed his red beard and then rose to fetch his bagpipes again. "Tensions grow, my lass. I hear of hostilities rising among our people against King Richard." Charles rubbed the chair leg beneath his bare foot.

"And I can't say that I'd blame them at all, for King Richard is merely strengthening English ties to France, no doubt." Charles wiped beads of sweat from his grizzly brow. "Yet, he is our King, and I, his royal knight, have been sworn to protect and support him."

He pushed away from the pottage, prepared to play a melody, hesitated, and added, "King Richard supports our efforts to share the Gospel in English. There is no doubt we must preserve his rein." With his pipes grazing his lips, he said, "I must play this nagging tune. It has been upon my breath for hours."

He played a border hymn as the sun rose while Nan sang.

The bleak ballad they finished darkened the early morning hour, leaving Saren doubtful.

Resting his instrument, Charles said, "Have you the air that you need to fill your lungs? Food to fill your stomach? Water to quench your thirst? These are a few questions to ask each night before you sleep. Because even if you wake before the dawn has broken, before the light of day, it may be too late." Charles licked his cracked lips, adding, "Whit's fur ye'll no go past ye."

Nan sang along to Charles's morning bagpipe serenades. Her rich voice boomed within the stone walls of the brothy. Saren oft sang along. Yet, on late mornings, her mouth only moved to the words, for Saren devoted all her intentions to listening to the sound. As powerful as her father's pipes, Nan's voice begged for her mum's reunion.

Saren rebraided her kinky curls and patted her puffy eyes. In that instant, listening to the music surrounding her, change loomed inevitable.

CHAPTER THREE

Nan's Song

Nan's song rose from an abysmal knowing that Saren yearned to explore for Nan was a fountain of wisdom of her Nan's and her Nan's Nan and so on. Many called her a witch and a gypsy, though she refused to predict one's fortune.

Nan often declared, "Never tell a fortune. Our fate is never written until we write it! We write our story as we live. We have our choices each moment. No doubt."

Villagers often came to Nan for medicines, herbs, and elixirs, mostly though they would come for her wisdom and advice.

As far as giving advice, she said, "Most people come seeking advice. They are lonely and want to be heard and empathized with. As far as taking advice, nobody is going to love you enough to set your course upon the seas by the *right, true, good stars*, except people that love you. Women are given the worst advice from all kinds of jealous women, or bored women, or false friends. Men giving women advice? Why? I'd listen to no one except your father. Other men, if they are taking much time to advise a young lady on any matter, I'm sure somewhere in their advice is that you remove some part of your dress!"

As she was chuckling and snapping a cloth at Saren, teasing her, Charles came in to carry on her studies, and Saren blushed deeply. "Oh, not your father, of course." She chuckled. Grinned, then showed a smile missing several teeth but still endearing. She was so full of laughter, always getting ready to bubble up.

Nan knew the plants to make you feel sleepy, the plants to make you feel strong and hardy after an illness. She knew the best tonics for a sore throat, which made you feel like you'd been given a magic elixir that cured every organ and limb of your body. Nan knew herbs that lifted your mood or filled you with energy and a spicy, milky tea full of intoxicating herbs that made your hair grow thick, full, and strong. "That's why yours is so strong and curly," she told Saren, "I've given you goat weed, moringa, rosemary, and nettle. That's what's in that tea with warm milk, honey, and cinnamon. I fixed you all the evenings of your and your mum's life."

She also knew tinctures and teas to help husbands and wives who couldn't have babies or to keep a baby in waiting till a mother had mended from the last one. This last tea was in huge demand, with Nan having to travel secretly to the royal palace several times yearly.

Yes, Nan was a wizard of cures and potions, for Saren's mother, had the most beautiful, long, and golden strawberry-colored hair. It curled in glowing falls of ringlets all about her face, and she, with a practiced art, would toss it off her face and back over her shoulders a hundred times a day, Saren remembered.

"Men," her mother had once told her. "They like a strong woman just fine. But it disturbs their sense of the balance of things in the world, and they need to feel they have control over *something* because they are the ones who must go and die in battle to rescue us from bears, fire, snakes, and floods. They must always be ready to give their lives for their loved ones while, as long as they're around, we get to live! So, don't be so hard on men who seem bossy or somehow rude – they must put on that brave face and muster a sense of control to prepare themselves for whatever battles await them today. . . you don't want to be their battle at home, too."

Nan added, "Aye. A fighting couple does nothing but exhaust each other to death. I'd almost rather die than live that life death that they live. And most don't live long . . . too busy arguing to hear the warning horns being blown! Not to mention all the subtle, quieter warnings of one's fate they must listen and watch for."

"What we're saying, Saren, is pick someone you love and can provide when you choose. None of us knows how long we have. Ensure you never waste your days in ways that don't bring you joy."

Remembering this, Saren vowed, "I won't marry till I find a love like Mother's and Father's—no matter what man Father wants me to marry to ease his worries about my future."

But Saren wondered if her mother could advise her now, seeing the state of her grandmother and Father, if she might tell her some kind of marriage might be wise or healthy, for all of them. *I'm too young to even know what to say to boys — especially men . . . or to lie with them...* Saren pitched her eyes shut.

Please, Lord, Saren prayed, *Can't I be a girl for just a little longer? Saren wanted* badly to retreat into songs, toys, games, good dreams, and every other aspect of her childhood that was quickly dissolving into the mist, like the doll she cherished that floated too far out to sea to ever catch when she fell asleep on the sandy, pebbly shore, waking too late for any hopes of retrieval.

"That's how grief is," Nan told Saren, "It never stops. It just changes shape and tones and moods as you change."

"You mean it gets bigger the older we get?" Saren asked fearfully.

"No. I mean the way stories change as you grow. The stories you hear as a child stay with you, but you experience them with an adult's mind and heart. We are always growing and changing, becoming better, more knowledgeable, and hopefully, more educated than we were the year before. And because we are growing and changing, we look back on these people we lost and see and understand them better and differently. It vexes me so. That's when I want to tell your mother something most. When I suddenly see why she got so angry about an issue one day. Then I'll admire her pride and steadfastness because I'll have had time to really reflect on it – and I'll be darned if I don't want to rush and find her and tell her I'm sorry."

"I feel that way all the time," Saren said.

"Well, tell her," Nan said, "You are a part of your mother. She will feel your feelings. Wherever her spirit roams. You can talk to her silently or aloud as you walk by the sea. I do it because I don't know what else to do with the words I need to say . . . and I miss chatting with her so constantly. I hadn't realized how our chatter kept the day lively 'till now."

Father played her mother's favorite happy songs on the good days. In this way, Saren learned that grief was like a winding river that ebbed and flowed, sometimes really moving and bubbling, occasionally quiet and placid.

These must have been the days when he felt far from his grief. He played the songs that always made Mother smile, dance, and laugh. Those days when her mother would grab Saren's hands, and they'd wheel around the brothy.

His faith in his ability to reach across time and space and be heard by her departed mother was a great comfort to Saren. She threw herself into that one leap of faith more than any other — as proof that she would, indeed, see her mother again. For *if her father,* so many times surrounded by death, watching soldiers die in the goriest way, or himself, fearing dying after a deep wound in battle—if he could believe that the spirit goes on after death, well, then, it must, most certainly be true, she hoped.

And hoped.

And hoped.

CHAPTER FOUR

A Decision Made

Tucking his pipes away, Charles spread a new goatskin across the settle. "Memory serves as your father's guide, luckily, since I've traveled to London many times. But that is a luxury you won't have, Saren. You must mark well everything I tell Ye — both mark them here," he said with two fingers pressing firmly on her right temple, "Here," he said, pointing to her heart, and "Here," he said, pointing to the piece of stretched goatskin he'd brought for the makings of a new map.

"We'll make you a strong and brightly writ map, my bonny lass. A very detailed one, with lots of landmarks.

Charles launched into new lessons with a brief review of the ones she knew too well. He spoke of the vast regions to the north, his forefather's homelands past Northumberland. All the male generations before him had fought over the pebbly shores long before he was born, and the many poor, unfortunate souls not gifted with royal blood or money enough to avoid the bloody battlefield.

He laughed and said again, "Your children's children may fight for this same heap of rocks, this cladach, as I. Aye, lass. It is our home and worth fighting for. But we have a more important purpose than that, even. We are to bring the word of God, and Jesus Christ crucified to all the world. It isn't fair that only people who speak Latin can read the most important book that will ever be of books. It is not Christian."

This is what her training was about. Together, they were to take one sacred book to London. Her father assured her that this book would be critical to the new translation of the Bible. Then, not only could everyone enjoy the word of God but the entire word of God—Saren was quickly beginning to see that this journey was very real and vital to the world.

They penned a new map together and weighed its four corners with small stones; her father made her trace her route and a backup route on the map. He asked her about what to do if the road was blocked by men of any kind . . . "Hide and always hide, for we don't often know who's really on our side," Saren recited.

"Aye, child," her father said.

"Where is it you must go should conflict or war arise?" "Here," Saren said, "London! Of course. We've talked about this for two years. But isn't this a *huge* city, as you say, with many small boroughs in it? So, *where in London?*"

"Tensions grow. And I can't say I blame them at all. King Richard made a horrible mistake in getting us so friendly with France. Some believe that's what caused the great plague, you know . . . our soldiers traveling there. But the marriage to a woman with no dowry and paying so extravagantly for her, that was no help with a public already giving most of their earnings to the Crown and going without food so the King could live lavishly and pay his wife's lavish dowry by marrying a peasant French woman."

"Yet, he is our King, and I, his royal knight, have been sworn to protect and support him. What is more, the King is very much in support of the Lollards and our efforts to help the English public enjoy a Bible they can read and understand themselves. I don't know that Bolly, Henry Bolingbroke, will if he's crowned. It's easier to preserve Richard's reign than to haggle a newly crowned king who just deposed a king and caused all that raucous into starting more struggle and strife in the realm," Charles finally took a breath of air.

"Father, where in London should I take the secrets? This is what I must know."

"Aye, girl! Of course." Charles retrieved a Lollard Bible from his belongings. "Here, Saren. You must find Father Sautrey at St. Othys' Cathedral. If you have problems or have haste, locate Jon the mute in London's city center. Jon knows of the secret book and how to help."

With her bright eyes seeking, shoulders back, and chin high, Saren questioned again, "I am now responsible and am entrusted with what magnificent secrets, Father?

Her father had become a knight to King Edward IV's council the year Saren was born. Father's sons would also have become knights of the council if they had lived. But all three sons had died during birth. Luckily, her mother lived, but she was sad for years and years, fearing she'd never have another child. Until Saren, and the last, a boy, took Mother's life with his own.

Saren was her mother's "Morning Star," her salvation, her promise of a new, better world after years of darkness.

"You know, Saren, it is as if you were destined for this journey since we decided to name you after my love for sea stars and your mother's reverence for Mother Mary." Your name means "God-given, that's the Mary part, and "sea star," that's the rest." The secret books contain a new revelation about a 13th disciple, the "Apostle to the Apostles— a *woman*."

"A woman?" Saren asked, "Really?"

"Aye, Lass, a woman named Mary but Mary Magdalena, perhaps. The seals are Coptic. We'll talk more about this later. I must concentrate on this map."

Today, her father seemed frantic with energy, unfinished tasks, and worry. She wondered if he'd received a message by pigeon.

The day seemed filled with menace, and the early spring winds arose with gusts and howls from the sea. "C'mon, Saren," her father commanded, "We should get to work. There's an evil storm on the horizon." They fueled their fire higher in the safety and cover of the stone brothy.

Salty air blew upon them from the sea beyond the house. No moat encircled to offer protection, and no fortress walls surrounded the perimeter. Simply, it was a high vantage point overlooking the sea to the north and west and the long open expanse of cobbled stone arriving to the east. Their home was two rooms of carved stone, unlike a peasant cottage, because of the family's knightly royal office: one room in which Saren and Nan shared a lone raised mattress of tow beneath a canopy to block the draft, and the other, the great room, where Father slept upon the settle once meals were cleared. This great room, with its stout table and warm fire, also gave a welcome place for their company to visit.

Charles ushered Saren about the house, describing and pointing out the provisions he had stockpiled in their reserves. "Fresh water is our most valuable asset here." Charles led Saren to the back where the wellhouse stood, shadowed by the cottage. We have plenty of seawater—but you cannot drink saltwater. It dries you out and makes you deathly ill and sick of mind in short.

"Don't even *think about it*," Saren finished for him.

Charles smiled. "Yes, so, guard the well with all your might; never abandon it. And when you arrive at a new place, locate the water well immediately." Walking back into the house, he pointed at the bucket. "Always have your bucket filled when you are home."

Charles marched to the larder just beyond their front door. He counted the perishable foods and meager supply of spices and candle wick. Then, he marched back seaward toward the bedroom to account for their woolen blankets and linens in Saren's mother's trunk of treasures. Saren stopped following once Charles's hand reached the chest at the base of her and Nan's bed. She remained there, waiting in the open door.

"Saren, are you paying heed?" he asked.

"Father, this is all knowledge that I already have. I know where things are kept. I have lived under your roof all my years." Without pause, Saren blurted, feeling awkward, "Since I may not see you . . . for . . some time, Father," she gulped, "please tell me . . . Why did you pick Mum? How will I know when I meet my Charles? How did you know, I mean, that she was 'the one'?" Tears touched her ivory cheek. She stepped outside, past the settle and the lingering warm coals of the kitchen's fire and sat on a lichen-covered stone to feel the fitful morning breeze as it escalated.

Counting the blankets, he had removed from the chest, Charles followed his daughter and her words, though not wanting to cease counting the family's inventory.

Still in thought, Saren continued, "You married Mom because you loved her. She was your world, your moon, and all your stars, as you put it . . . your *bhoidheach ghaoil*. You always told me so. That was why you married her." Tears sprinkled from her black lashes as Charles knelt to one knee. He rested his massive, callused hands atop Saren's.

"Yes, Saren. That is why I married your mom, my beautiful love." He shook his shaggy head in wonderment of her aim.

"Then that is why I shall marry. Because I'm loved like that." Tears streamed, followed by sobs. "I will never marry a man out of fear for my welfare. You cannot ever make me, Father, never." Saren rose close to Charles, nearly knocking her father backward with her abruptness. "I overheard you telling Nan of finding me a suitor."

Charles, a large, stout man, rose before his tiny daughter, his head hung low, shuffling his bare foot on the ground. "I fear for your future, my daughter. Without me, you are vulnerable." He raised her face to see her eyes. "I am only thinking of your safety, your protection, Saren." He took a labored breath, reluctant to speak, but said, "Aye, lass, as your father, I must ensure that you are to be cared for properly before… before I return to duty." His words were forced.

Saren would not look into her father's eyes. She gnawed her lower lip. "What duty, Father? What are you returning to? Tell me, Father, that you know King Richard will not find alliance with the wild Irish. Please tell me, Father, that you will not go but always remain here safe with me and Nan." She dropped back to her rocky seat and dropped her tiny hands to her side.

"Saren, my duty to return to King Richard's command is inevitable. We do not know our departure, but I must leave you prepared when I must." Charles caught her eyes.

Saren reached toward him, then took his hands back in her own. "What about love, Father? What about that?" She dropped her gaze once more and shook her head as if to clear the mist from the ocean waves heard crashing just steps beyond the house.

Saren stood tall, squeezing his hands. "I am no more a child and too old to be taken in by another family, even though I look young." Saren's eyes reflected the twinkle of the lingering stars. "But, Father, I am strong and agile. And I have Nan," she assured him as she recognized her grandmother's silhouette approaching along the cobbled road. Saren rushed to help her with her kindling basket of fuel for their fire, their skirts flowing with the movement of their steps.

Sidling next to Nan, Saren desperately sought support with her pleading eyes. "Charles, Saren has me and always will."

The older woman smiled knowingly at her granddaughter and nudged her with an elbow as if her knitting caused it. "Her future life as an adult is hers to write, not yours, and she has just as much right to find all the love in the world – all the romance and silliness and magic you did with her mother. And I know you know that she's meant to do important things all by herself in this world. She's meant to discover her purpose in life before she begins living solely for her husband and child, as *all women should. All men too.*" She sighed, exasperatedly and loud, "but alas, not many men allow their wives or womenfolk to experience freedom and are so intimidated by wit, intelligence, and beauty they want to chain it down, saddle it with a brood of children, and plant a flag on it as if people could possibly be owned or stashed away like property any more than a woman's mind or soul can."

Nan closed her eyes and whispered a prayer, "I am song to the last; I am fear and bright; I am a serpent; I am reverence." She smiled to her granddaughter, for the two women shared a connection stretching backward and forward. They knew each other as spirits, without bodies or ages. Their souls spoke before she was ever born, she often thought. Nothing ever needed to be explained, not even the complex personal things. She already knew and conveyed this knowledge to Saren with her eyes – no matter what the subject.

Although talk between them often stayed upon the day-to-day things, if she was hurting or troubled, her grandmother stayed close to her. Out of a need for them both to find peace, as neither could rest until the other found *some kind of comfort* before going to sleep. One of their family's most seriously clutched beliefs and rules was that you never go to bed on an argument because sleep brings forth all truths and secrets. It's better to bring them out yourselves and not risk horribly cathartic and painful dreams where your nightmares punish you.

Charles shook his red beard and winked at Nan, saying, "Very well, child." He rose and went into the house to the opposite corner of the main room, past the settle, to his leather-bound trunk. He retrieved a whalebone bow leaning in the corner behind it. Stringing the sinew tight, he commanded, "Saren, it is time, then." A decision was made. He returned to face the doorway, waiting for Saren to enter their home. "I have been teaching you ever since you could walk. Now, let us begin your formal training to use a weapon." Smiling, he commanded again, "Saren. Lead the way to the meadow." He rested his open hand upon her shoulder, followed her out, and shut the door behind them.

CHAPTER FIVE

Solemn Duty

The bow was much heavier than it appeared. Saren held it up and away, struggling not to wobble under its weight as the winds pushed her.

"This bow is too big for you, but if you can master this, you will shoot almost anything," Charles said quietly. They had strolled to the outermost meadow, away from peoples' eyes and wonderment as the sun climbed higher and the winds from the sea calmed. Charles watched, alert to thieves lurking not so far from the village.

Saren pulled the bow's sinew string as far as her tiny arms allowed. She aimed at a fir tree and fired, losing her arrow in the thicket beyond. In the waxing sunlight, the duo searched the forest floor for her lost arrow. After several attempts, she finally lodged an arrow into a trunk. Her one small success spurred further successes.

"Your first day of archery was successful, Saren. Let us head for home and pottage. Perhaps daylight tomorrow will help us locate the missing arrow," Charles said as the fading light of day left them unable to locate the one arrow lost.

The studies at home continued. Saren was eager to have her father read as she sat before him on the floor of packed earth in the great room where the home's fire warmed them.

Reading into the night, they used the last of their candle's wick, or they would have continued with her studies. "I shall find us more candlewick tomorrow," Charles answered his daughter's unasked question.

"But Father. How shall you pay? We have no money left after taxes and tithing." Saren rose from the table, scraping the pooled wax into a crock to be melted and shaped anew. "The Church takes all we have." She spoke the truth.

"No need to worry tonight, my girl. We can manage better by the light of day." Charles removed his tunic and sat across the settle nearby.

"I know you wonder, my lass, why the king sends me forth each week." Charles rose, wiped a lanoline rag across the dry whalebone bow, and replaced it to stand behind his trunk. "I promise to tell you everything I learn of my upcoming assignments as soon as I know. For now, I'm overjoyed to be teaching you to fire a bow." His handsome smile was contagious—the more he spoke of teaching Saren, the larger he grinned, as did Saren.

"Not only is this my solemnly sworn duty to King Richard, Saren, but King Richard is our only hope for continuing to spread the English Bibles." Charles's smile weakened as he reclaimed his place on the settle. "Though the English Bibles remain illegal, our King does nothing to enforce laws restricting our movement. He encourages and supports our works with financial support from his mother, Joan of Kent."

With a heavy sigh, he added, "King Richard does not always send me away." Charles's voice cracked. "Our Earl here in Northumberland, Lord Percy, has ordered me to attend this upcoming Irish expedition. Some things must be done to protect our King." Father now spoke behind a forced smile. "Because of the involvement of the Church, King Richard must keep a distance from many of our arrangements. The King, his mother, and many council members support our work to share English Bibles. The Church, of course, condemns them." He sighed. "We have much work at hand in protecting our King, for without his support of our endeavors, the Church retains all control of the people, our money, and our souls. I promise not to leave you ill-prepared."

Saren did not respond to her father's words then. There would be another time for that. She had always been proud of her father's rank and place among the royal knights, but the days were different for a girl on the brink of womanhood. She understood that the winds were shifting.

Night's wind blew in from the sea and hurled an onslaught of pebbles against the stone house. The percussion on the oak-planked door roused Charles from his fitful dreams of battle and haste, anger, and betrayal.

He rose to fan the last glowing coals and fuel the house's small fire. Filling the kettle over the embers with water to heat and opening the door to the lady's bedroom to allow warmth to enter, the memory of his night's dream ravaged upon him with foggy dread, like the sandy pebbles striking their home.

Dreams seldom visited Charles's sleep. When he did spend any moments beyond wakefulness, his nights were usually quiet and peaceful. Having spent a restless and fitful night filled with vivid and horrific details of the battle, Charles's unease boiled as the kettle now did.

He removed the scalding pot as the same nagging ballad wormed back into his mind, and he hummed:

"This began on Cheviot the hills abune Early on a Monday;

By that it drew to the hour of noon A hundred fat harts dead there lay."[1]

Charles failed to recall having ever had such grimacing terrors visit his sleep. The last night's turmoil would leave a wretched taste in his mouth throughout the day. Watching the glowing coals, he tried to recollect each detail as it had unfolded, though the harder he tried to remember the dream, the farther gone it seemed. Only Charles's bitterness at his old friend Lord Percy's presence in his dream remained. As the tune within his skull continued:

"They blew a mort upon the bent, They' sembled on ides shear;

To the quarry then the Percy went To the brittling of the deer."[2]

And this ugliness quickly transformed into what he could feel were unusual leg cramps. Cramps that he could do nothing to quell; spasms near his pelvis that he had never experienced before doubled him over and forced him to sit in an awkward cross-legged position to continue stoking the ever-growing fire.

The cramps, the dream—they were somehow connected. Charles rocked to and fro there upon the packed earth before the fire. The women had not yet risen, and he shut his eyes, hearing the tempo of the waves crashing below upon the crags. Memories of the battle dream, though real, stirred at last. Memories of his old friend and comrade Lord Percy there on the battlefield, murdering and laughing as he killed. He took and robbed from all that departed, unlike any memories of the active battle he had experienced alongside his old friend. Charles would soon regret dismissing this warning that visited his dream and body.

As the fire warmed the home, Charles lost all interest in his dreams that had only moments prior gripped his heart. As rapidly as the pain had subsided, so did his need to explain the dream.

◈   ◈   ◈

CHAPTER SIX

Barwick-upon-Tweed

Hints of spring came upon them, a day when snow crystals melted before reaching the earth. Saren and her Father gathered with a crowd of elderly men and younger lads on the outskirts of Barwick-upon-Tweed, a two-day carriage ride north from their brothy. There were smiles, firm handshakes, and roughened embraces despite the hungry and weary hearts among them. The conversation was positive. They followed a hefty man dressed in a friar's frock to a small church tucked among the trees. The building was cold and dark when they arrived, smelling of caged air. Charles helped light candles around the room. Saren sat against the wall close to the door to keep from being trampled.

Like their home, the Church was made of squared stones strategically stacked to leave windows for light. *One could just reach a hand through had there not been tapestries upon them, or fire an arrow from Father's whalebone bow if the need should arise,* Saren thought.

Father led the group of men in a short sermon. She knew him to be a Lollard Priest—a poor priest for the people and for God. He read passages from their Lord's book, "Another parable put he forth unto them, saying, The Kingdom of heaven is likened unto a man which sowed good seed in his field: But while men slept, his enemy came and sowed tares among the wheat, and went his way..."[3] Father looked at each man in the Church and then closed his book.

"These are the words that shall be reiterated to us. But, my brethren, we know the truth and that the Church is twisting the Lord›s word to justify their own greed. The truth shall be heard far and wide." Father spoke on in the candle›s glow. Saren sat on listening with wide eyes. Knowing her father and his ideals, this was the first time she had heard him speak so in a public place among like-minded men, all of whom were listening to him read from a forbidden Bible.

"The field is the world; the good seed are the children of the kingdom, but the tares are the children of the wicked one; As therefore the tares are gathered and burned in the fire; so, shall it be in the end of this world,"[4] Father read again from Wycliffe's complete translations of the Latin Vulgate cradled in his hands. Then he raised his head and spoke. "Our King Richard supports all of our Lollard doings while the Church opposes them; you understand?" Father wiped the sweat dripping from his brow, though his breath could be seen in the candle's glow. "The Lollard Society must unite and support our King Richard to see our Bibles shared in English. Or in Welsh. Or in Irish or any other native language that people understand beyond Latin," he added. "We shan't be forced to pay tithing in exchange for forgiveness of sins read to us in a language we can't understand. It is criminal." Charles held his breath as he spoke, "Cannot you wonder what other words of the Lord are being repressed from us?"

Saren would forever remember her father's hands, cracked and swollen, beneath his warn book. His heart broken.

The men shuffled out of Northumberland's undisclosed Holy Trinity parish church into the twilight and said farewells.

Though she had listened to every word her father had spoken through the candlelight, questions poured from her lips. "Father, who were these men today? Why did you speak so ill of the Church? What children are to be burned in the fire?" Saren plead.

Charles stood firm, holding his daughter's hands, listening to her request without smiling. Turning, he glanced behind his shoulder, perhaps to ensure no other would hear him say, "No children will burn in the fire, girl. I promise to always be near, in spirit when not in body, to keep you safe." Though a chill lingered in the air, Charles wiped his forehead. "A battle, I am sure, is looming. France is on King Richard's side and supports our Lollard movement. If God or the King summons, I want you to be armed with all you might need." His shoulders slumped as he continued to speak. "I believe some men among us oppose our efforts and are hastening change." Stopping, Charles took Saren's hands in his and added, "You are right. I am sorry for my fatherly request that you should marry. That would be for me, not you. Never marry a man unless he loves you. Loves you like the world."

"And the moon and the stars?" Saren giggled, wiping her damp eye.

"Yes, like the moon and the stars."

She turned to look at the moss-covered earth. "I am proud of what you do, Father. But I shall not marry for my safety. Not ever. I am strong and fast. I may not be allowed to be a knight of King Richard's court, but I can be a rebel knight." Saren grinned.

"Aye, spoken like a true warrior," Charles sighed. "Very well, then. You are my daughter. Though you may grow hungry and tired." Charles cupped Saren's small face in his hand, "We must work silently and discretely."

Saren gripped her father's arm as they prepared to find lodging for their night's stay in the port city. The duo would be visiting the port tomorrow to receive goods and supplies arriving there for their King.

CHAPTER SEVEN

Going To Port

The dawn came early. Saren was startled awake by the slamming of a door and her father's voice beyond the tapestry surrounding her straw mattress.

The travelers were offered little conversation at the fellow Lollard's cottage the night prior, nor any hints of a meal. The morning brought forth tempting scents of pottage or gruel, causing her empty tummy to roust her to her feet.

Wiping the sleep from her eyes, she cursed for absently leaving her hairbrush behind.

Saren managed to smooth her wild locks and secure her long braid upon her head in a presentable coil.

Urgent to relieve her bladder, she entered the cottage to ask where the nearest garderobe might be.

The hearty priest that provided their lodging, quick with answers, grabbed Saren by the wrist and escorted her beyond the cottage door to the nearby toilet.

The sunrise masked beyond rooftops, was nothing like sunrises near her Alnwick home. There hung an ugly cloak of smoot upon the breeze. Smells Saren could not identify, nor did she find any desire to do so.

Saren hurried about her necessitates and quickly returned to the cottage, grateful for the warm meal and flat mead.

Though intentionally focused on her morning meal, Saren listened to her father and his fellow Lollard priest's conversation. The men continued the conversation from the Parish Church. "There remain, for too many nights, and privileges denied us by the Church. Hence by the Crown," Charles spoke.

"Augh, it is all a declaration of powers to be controlled. As the Crown struggles to control the masses, The Church simply chooses to deny us," the priest added. "All the while, dear friend, as you retrieve your goods from the port, you are welcome here another night if the need arises."

"I thank Ye wholeheartedly. Kind Sir," replied Charles. We shall see how our day follows. Come, Lass. We shall venture onward."

Without another moment lost, Saren and her Father gathered their belongings. They navigated away from the cozy cottage and into the busy port town of Barwick-Upon-Tweed. The duo strode with purpose and dignity. Saren, her head high while breathing shallow breaths to avoid the decaying smells of rotting fish and human waste.

She held loosely, yet strong, to her father's crooked arm as he stepped purposely along the planked walk above the refuse.

"We are looking for the Galleon, Al-Aour from Alexandria. She is an Egyptian warship, no doubt, dear child. I am begging our merciful father, we haven't the necessity to buy a pay-pony for no doubt our fanciful King has made none other than a lavish request from abroad."

The horizon, lined with sail less ships, clustered with bobbing vessels, while the port below was lined with vibrantly colored flags and crews of varying sizes.

Letting loose of Saren's gentle clasped hand, Charles approached a tall, dark-skinned, and well-decorated man as he finished giving stern orders to his young crew.

The tall sailor, looking Charles at eye level, never offered a nod nor a smile, yet simply pointed back the way they had walked.

Shaking his long, loose head of stark red hair, Charles approached Saren as she waited, rooted to the creaking port planks.

Charles smiled confidently and reclasped her arm, "Ay, we shall retrace our few steps and search the boats docked to the south. Come along."

Having walked nearly an hour upon the planked walk, they located the great Al-Aoura dingy and half her ore's men. The ship's captain, dressed in an ornate red silk tunic and an ivory silk turban, draped his head past his shoulders. Shouting orders to his oarsmen in what Saren recognized as Arabic. His cheerful smile never left his lips or his seat from the warm trunk he sat upon.

Charles approached the elderly man with his hands open and his head high.

A young oarsman leaped between the two men. A striking smile resembling the ship's captain was undeniable. His eyes, though, a cool blue, captured Saren's and remained there.

The elderly captain slowly rose to his feet, raising his hand in acceptance and gentle affirmation to the protective youth.

His eyes never leaving Saren's.

The captain and Charles conversed then in English as the young oarsman approached Saren with his hand extended in greeting.

Saren received his callused, warm hand in a gentle glasp as she gazed toward her father with uncomfortable eyes.

The young man's English was refined compared to her homeland's dialect, keeping her intrigued as he offered his welcome and introduction. "My name is Ali; I am the ship's captain, Joseph's son and his first mate, at your service," his smile crooked, leaving a small dimple at the edge of his mouth.

Saren's smile grew as she was intrigued by the young man's refinement.

The two fathers conversed only a moment more before her father approached, explaining, "We shall return to the market and locate a wagon, for we have a fine load of silks, spices, and iron to return to Alnwick Castle, Saren. Once we've secured our transit home, we shall row out to the ship and load the dingy with our goods."

"Alas, Father," Saren smiled and breathed the salty, smelly air."

"Sit with me, an old sailor soul, Child, while your Father and Ali return to the city center."

Saren's father clutched her hand and nodded. And he and her new acquaintance left her sitting near the dingy with the aged sailor to wait. She had yet to sit upon the plank crate before Joseph began telling of the voyage up the coast and the early summer storm they had encountered. "I hope you are not hungry, girl," he said with a hearty laugh. "You, see?" his smile broadened. "My larder is back at the ship." With a tip of his head, he added, "How long shall you and your father remain here at The Barwick?" And without waiting for Saren to reply, he offered, "If you must stay over again, we've plenty of empty beds upon the Al-Aoura, no doubt, as many of our passengers shan't return home this eve.

Saren sat, her shoulders facing sideways to the captain, avoiding the late morning sun's direct blaze. She rummaged in her satchel to locate the lightest book in her belongings to raise above her bow and provide shade from the intense rays.

"What book are you reading, Woman?" Captain Joseph asked as he studied the bland tapestry covering her sunshade book.

"Oh! Thus, Saren lowered her father's book to retrieve the title, knowing the direction this forbidden book that she selected would steer their later conversations.

"These are translations that my father is working on," Saren paused as she carefully chose the language to align with the captain's spirituality.

"Aye, Woman. Your father, then, is he German in origin?"

"No, Sir. Simply studies the translations."

"Deutsch ist keine schöne sprache zum lernen." Smiling, Joseph repeated, "German is not a pretty language to study, you see. What other languages does your father study in the Bible?" The captain stooped into Saren's bag, touching the book she had placed there.

Struggling, she offered, "My father reads in Latin, Greek, Scottish, Cornish, French, and English, that is all."

"Augh! No Hebrew. Hebrew and Coptic are the two languages in which the true Bible was written. I advise him to learn Hebrew and Coptic to understand scripture completely."

"Why, of course, he should. I shall advise. Thank, Ye."

"Woman, when we return to the Al-Aour, I shall give you a gift for you to begin your Hebrew studies. Coptic, you should remain on our ship and return to Alexandria to master." Rising from his wooden seat, Joseph stretched his back, his hands loosely pressing his hips as he straightened his spine.

"Loksy here," Joseph pointed to her father and his son, walking towards them smiling.

"They must have undoubtedly found success, don't you agree?" He offered his hand to help her to her feet.

CHAPTER EIGHT

The Red Seal of His Adorable One

Joseph, his son Ali, Saren, and her father all maneuvered into the dinghy. Eight young oarsmen followed, and the small boat was soon heading toward the great warship, rocking upon its resting place upon the horizon.

Aboard the Al-Aoura, the remaining sailors effortlessly hoisted them aboard.

A dark-haired boy, not more than five, scurried to stand near Saren's side. His smile broad, eyes matching, he took Saren's hand in his own and showed no interest in letting go.

"Ay, Lady. He likes you. I see that you have met our cabin boy, Matthew. Come now," Joseph hollered, summoning the deck crew together. "We have goods for King Richard to be ferried to shore, alas," he roused his crew and gave orders to more lads.

Saren settled herself upon the rocking vessel and witnessed the chore of gathering the goods, which was made effortless by the quick crew.

"Dear girl," Charles snuck from behind. It is going on late in the day. It's too late to get traveling home, I reckon. We shall remain here for the night and be ferried back to shore at dawn," he smiled and pattered her knee as he left to accept Joseph's invitation.

The dinner bell rang as the late afternoon sun perched upon the sea's western horizon.

Joyful boys and a few men gathered around the firebox upon the deck.

"This is a celebration dinner," Joseph exclaimed. "Our crew has not enjoyed a hot meal in weeks. And those that have gone on to shore are missing our bounty," he spooned hot lentils onto wooden platters and sent his little deck boy one to deliver to Saren and one for her father.

Mead shared among the boys as they waited for their platters and meandered about to locate an empty place to enjoy the hot meal.

Joseph finished serving his crew, and the fire was quickly buried beneath the sands of the box and closed. He came and sat near Charles, ready to enjoy his own dinner.

"Not a meal for a King, yet a meal for his delivery men," Joseph smiled, raising his mug of staling mead in toast, "and delivery woman," he nodded a smile to Saren.

"Thank Ye, Sir." Saren smiled as her tummy grumbled. "This is tasty indeed."

"Ay, Woman. Tis over salty as such are the ways upon the sea." Joseph hurried to eat his meal while it was hot.

Ali, his son, stood and came and sat nearer, asking, "Charles, do you have some reading for us and the crew this evening? Surely, you have some book that we," he pointed around to the eager crew, "would enjoy."

Still eating his meal, Charles nodded in agreement and pointed to his satchel with a nod. "Ay, Lad. There in my satchel are plenty to partake for your liking." Charles then continued his meal and carried on in conversation with Joseph.

The meal was devoured momentarily, and the crew was about their chores. Some secured their own ship while others secured Saren and her father's load aboard the dingy as Ali approached Joseph, Charles, and Saren with her father's open satchel and bound secret book.

"Charles, you have yet to read this," he stepped forward, setting Charles's secret book upon Joseph's lap. "The unbroken seal upon it is Coptic, no doubt."

Saren's eyes widened as she held her breath, watching for her father's reaction.

"Ay," Charles rose. Those books are bound for safekeeping," he smiled.

"I see, and how are ye to protect that you do not know, Sir? What are they, and why do they have Coptic symbols upon them? Father, what does this say?" Ari asked, pointing to the red seals melted upon the cover.

"Ali, these are the King's and private. You might lose your fingers for retrieving them from another's satchel," Joseph barked yet caressed the fancy marking.

"That is fine, Joseph," Charles defended. "These books are not the King's, and I agreed to read this evening. However, I do not know what they say, nor have they been opened."

"Would you like to know what they say, Charles? I can read the Coptic seal," Joseph replied, smiling at Saren, his brow raised in wonder. "For this is the red seal of His treasure . . . His Adorable One, Mary. His 13th disciple."

The red seal of his adorable one, Mary, you say?. "I do know this. Yes, please read them." Charles winked at Saren and offered her his gentle smile. His smile that she had not seen in the weeks since her mother and baby brother passed.

Joseph smiled and clapped his hands, unable to deny his excitement reading ancient texts and such mysterious works.

He rose and approached Charles for private consort. The ancient book preserved within Father's leather satchel rested bound in crisp leather beneath the other Bibles and documents of his possession.

Charles held the leather-bound book, his fingers touching Joseph's as he passed the book to him with a comforting nod of approval.

The seal and laces of the ancient book were removed. Yet, the brittle papyrus pages were bound together and too fragile to separate effortlessly.

Saren held her breath.

"How many generations has this book been in your family's care?" Joseph asked, noticing the fragile task of loosening the leather binding.

"As many fathers and grandfathers as I can count, dear friend. The book, or books, were a gift to Princess Enflaed, our grandfather's aunt from St. Paulinus, on her baptismal day. I have not dared open the binding knowing that the symbol is of Mary, I feared its destruction."

"This is good; it is preserved nicely for a thousand years, no doubt," Joseph observed.

"One thousand years at the least, I am certain, Joseph. What more can you tell of the symbols?" Charles asked.

"Charles, Saren, Ali. The most beautiful symbols. Coptic, indeed, are translations from Greek, I see. Aye, this book is a copy then and not the only one in existence, I pray," Joseph smiled. "Perhaps these pages are copied, yes. Where the originals exist shall remain a mystery," Joseph added.

The ship rocked, the sea lapped upon the old warship's hull, and the meager crew resting on the deck sat silently, witnessing the light fade from the sky. Candles were fetched as the quiet grew comfortable upon them.

Joseph spoke to Charles as though the two men, now, were the only two upon the ship. Saren and Ali maneuvered closer.

"The Beginning is the Gospel of Mary." And with a heavy sigh, Joseph explained, "There appear many pages torn away and removed from the beginning," he explained.

"The Savior said," Joseph coughed quietly. "All nature, all creatures live in and with one another, and all nature returns to their roots."[5]

Licking his dry lips once, Joseph continued, "He who has ears to hear, let him hear. What is the sin of the world?"[6]

Wrinkling his brow in curiosity, Joseph read what he could decipher, *"… are you who make a sin. This is why the Good came into your world, to return the world to its root."*

Looking at the shadowed faces among the listeners, Joseph read, *"That is why you suffer and die, for you are deprived of the One who can heal you. He who has a mind to understand, let him understand."*[7]

Movement among the listeners encouraged Joseph to pause his reading. "This book is a priceless treasure; I will spend the hours of the night reading and into the dawn for as long as you, Charles, and your daughter can remain. Yes, there is much I can not read, I fear… I will do my best."

Ali then pushed Saren's satchel toward her, "Can you write some that he reads in English for me, Ma'am, please?"

"Aye, and for me," Saren agreed, removing her tablet and ink bottle from her belongings.

The middle pages are bound shut. I read these markings of the apostle John, also in salicylic Coptic. I cannot read all these nor do harm to the document. So, only the loosened pages shall suffice," Joseph read on.

"These are the teachings of the Savior and the unraveling of the mysteries of all things hidden,"[8] Joseph read.

"The Pharisee, Arimanius said to him, where is your master whom you followed? The Savior said, "He has gone to the place from which he came."[9]

The following pages opened easily, and Joseph read on, *"John, John, you doubt. You are afraid. You are not unknowing of what you see are you? Do not be scared! I am the one who is with you always. I am the Father, I am the Mother, I am the Son. I have come to teach you what is and what was, and what will come to pass."*[10]

The crew on the decks listened as the night's breeze rocked the sleepy vessel. Joseph rested upon a closed trunk with candles flickering around him.

"John asked to know it, and the Savior said to him, "The Monad is a monarchy with nothing above it. It is he who exists as God of everything, the Invisible one who is above everything, who is pure light of which no eye can look."[11]

Pages again were stuck together. Joseph paused to loosen the next and read, *"For the perfection is majestic. He is pure, immeasurable mind."*[12]

Snores echoed from the ship's hull, and the listeners lingering shared their candles.

Saren struggled to keep her eyes from closing as Joseph read on about the confusing Coptic marks of John the Apostle when he stopped a moment to refill his goblet and stretch his legs.

"There remain so many hours of reading and research here, good sir," Joseph advised Charles as he turned the delicate pages. Leaning forward, he read, "The Sophia of

Jesus Christ. Yes, this is what the Coptic symbols tell. The Sophia of Jesus Christ."

"After he rose from the dead, his twelve disciples and seven women continued to be his followers and went to Galilee onto the mountain called "Divination and Joy.""[13]

"This mountain," Saren interrupted Joseph's reading. Her voice sprinkled starlight like the twinkling reflections upon the lapping sea below. "This mountain is but the journey of seeking through God. Divination. Not a mountain called Divination?" she asked clearly.

Without waiting for a response from the others, she went on. "Life is to be lived in joyous divination and seeking."[14]

The dawn rose upon them in subtle light as the weary crew emerged from the hull. The night's reading ceased, yet talks continued, discussing a plan for loading the ferry boat.

"We must stop with our translations. Sad as I will be for ceasing, I am ever grateful and joyous to have read some of your secret treasures," Joseph said, rubbing his weary eyes and yawning deeply. "Kind Sir, if I may ask, what is your plan to preserve and protect such treasures from falling to the Roman Church? For, you know, as I, they will demand its destructions."

"Aye. I know this; the Church, though, does not know what I have. Entirely."

"Nor do you, Dear Charles of Northumberland. This reading of later is just a sample of what truths live here among these papyrus pages." For here, the next symbol that I decipher of the Sophia of Jesus Christ translates into, 'The underlying reality of the universe and the plan.'"[15]

Smiling, Joseph pulls his grandson close. "Ali, let us help our new friends on the road."

The dingy was loaded with goods and set with crew toward shore. Saren waved her fare-thee-wells and was rocked to sleep as the smaller vessel landed upon the docks.

Grateful for the oarsmen for escorting the King's lavish cargo to shore and aboard their borrowed wagon. Saren offered Joseph her hand and hugged him about his waist.

Leaning over her, he whispered, "Woman, if ever you need, come to Alexandria, and you will find the Al-Aoura upon the docks. There is where you will find your friends. And remember there is much more to translate and more to transcribe. Travel now in God's Graces and for always," Joseph said as he placed a worn Coptic Bible in Saren's clasp and kissed her upon the forehead.

CHAPTER NINE

Pilgrimage home from Barwick

The stars overhead attempted to outshine each other. No moon filled the sky, and when it did appear, it was bright enough to cast their shadows. Charles and Saren traveled into the night, listening for thieves lurking.

As they approached a clump of trees, Saren pointed ahead to a lone rider who slunk into the forest like smoke at dusk. "Should we wait a spell here or keep on?" She hesitated.

"Press on, dear. He looks to be in a hurry away from you and me. I imagine he's as scared of us as we are of him." Charles walked on, holding the cart horse close by its hemp halter, thus keeping his daughter close.

"The Lollard Knights, King Richard's Knights as we have been called, have traveled as far as southern France. Did you know, Saren, that we have the support of King Charles there?" Father chuckled, his laughter easing her fears of the lonely passage home.

As they slowed before a creek, Saren leaped down to walk along and nearer her father.

Charles grabbed for Saren's hand and stopped. He waited for her to match his pace and for him to catch his breath.

"But Father. Why is this funny? The peaceful relation between England and France—if we are peaceful with France, why is there so much unease here among our own?" her brows furrowed.

"Why the worry of battle? I laugh, my girl because it was the marriage of a French princess to our English King Edward that began the wars of one hundred years. And another marriage of the same matching is what has ended it. Is not that a comedy?"

Charles clasped Saren's hand again as they marched down the road, ignoring her second question.

Charles looked to the worn, cobbled road beneath their feet, "Saren, I need you to carry on for me." He stopped in the path and sighed. "If I am called away, please promise me that you will protect the family's treasured book. It is the greatest burden a father could imagine passing down to his child, but I cannot take them with me if I'm called away. I must leave this book and its secrets in your care for their safekeeping." Charles gnawed his lower lip as he added, "If you do become fearful, or if I do not return as planned, then take the book to London and deliver it to Father Sautrey at St. Othys' Cathedral." A comforting smile spread behind his ginger-whiskered face. "Our family was entrusted with these manuscripts, and now that they have been opened, you have my blessing to translate and transcribe what you find." He closed her hands upon his own. "Keep them wrapped securely in the leather binding and within this leather satchel, and they will be protected from the elements. If the need arises, I have stashed enough coin in your mother's wooden vase for your passage and two weeks' lodging."

Saren held her breath longer than intended and exhaled with a great gasp, "Father, I am but a girl. How can I accomplish such a task?" Sighing and kicking her worn shoe, she added, "A knightly task… you've given me a task." She smiled. "I promise, Father."

They walked hand in hand. Saren's mind raced with questions and concerns. She gnawed her lower lip with worry, and the weight of responsibility she now carried on her shoulders grew heavier with each step.

"All animals, species, and the like. We all live with one another and will then die and be resolved back into our own roots. I think that is how Joseph began last evening," Saren finally spoke. I am inspired to read my notes as soon as possible."

"That is a splendid idea, though stopping and camping on this road at night is not an option, Saren. Keep moving. Moving will help inspire your memory. It does mine." Charles smiled. "And yes, he did say that we all creatures exist with one another together and die, I reckon, back into the roots of its individual nature. Charles explained again. He also said, "There is no sin, but what we make sinful."

Keeping up with her father's stride, Saren smiled now and stepped along the road, alert and brimming with questions. "The Monad who is God, the invisible One. It is neither male nor woman and just is. Is pure immeasurable light."

"Exactly Saren. And I remember from the Apocryphon of John. Perfection is a majestic and pure, immeasurable mind. Today's Church fears the people to have pure, immeasurable minds of their own. Any mind for that matter."

As they neared their cottage, Charles was the first to notice the fire's glow coming from within. "Hurry, Saren," Joseph pulled the cart horse to quicken his hooves upon the cobblestone road.

Nan has the evening fire ablaze." They rushed toward the light.

The cool spring breeze from the sea graced Saren's skin. The salty air of the sunbaked Earth lingered, like her questions about the contents of the secret manuscripts she now bore. Her heartbeat quickened as she remembered Joseph's words and the divination that she now embarked on.

Nan spooned her bowl of pottage from the kettle, set it upon the settle, and stood behind her chair. Saren and

Charles sat with spoons, ready to partake of the hearty meal, though they waited for the old crone to give her blessing.

"Lord an' Lady…" She shut her eyes. "Grant us thy river of water, to accept what we cannot change. The power of fire, fer energy an' courage to change thy things that we can." She opened her eyes. Smiling, she continued. "Thy power of air, for thy ability to know thy difference. Lord an' Lady, grant us thy power of Earth, for thy strength to know an' walk our path."[16]

They sat around the settle and ate their meal together. Saren took her father's hand as he relaxed afterward and felt his palm's worn, tough skin. She knew he had been transcribing Bibles late into the dark hours, which was why they were often without enough wick for their candles.

He also would walk the ever-long stretches of beach for countless sunrises and sunsets. Now, his body slimmed more, revealing the many meals she and Nan had partaken in without his company as the spring season slowly hinted at summer's return.

Nan, alert to Charles's dismay, attempted to lighten his mood. "Charles, your wisdom is far beyond the times. Perhaps our history is your redeemer?" She smiled.

Father, though, did not return her smile. He asked, "Our Pagan history, Nan? That is always yer solution."

"Why, yes, Charles." In her haggard and booming voice, Nan recited Mother Earth's prayer:

"Earth, divine goddess, Mother Nature who generates all things an' brings forth anew the sun which you have given to the nations; Guardian of sky an' sea and of all gods an' powers an' through yer power all nature falls silent an' then sinks in sleep. An' again you bring back the light an' chase away night an' yet again you cover us most securely with yer shades. You contain chaos infinite, yes, an' winds an' showers an' storms; you send 'em out when ye will an' cause thy seas to roar; you chase away thy sun an' arouse the storm."[17]

Father and Saren listened to Nan's words. Though neither voiced agreement, Saren did witness a smile touch her father's lips.

However, His smile disappeared as Nan continued, "The secrets you possess shall be your destruction, Charles. You ought to destroy them if you cannot keep them safe."

"Nan, the book or the three books we now know, is our family's burden. To carry until the season is appropriate for their revelation. I will not destroy them."

"I see, Charles," Nan agreed. "I believe the words hidden in those papyrus pages bridge the worlds across history, across our faiths an' our Gods our Goddesses," Nan rose and began clearing the settle. "Charles, I foretell those secrets will turn a grander war than the one swiftly approaching."

"Perhaps, dear Nan. That is not my burden now." With his gloom returned, Father did not voice his dread of impending opposition. His details were of little use, for everything he believed to be approaching was, as he told, "only his premonition." Had he dreamt of impending battle? Had someone warned him? He would not tell.

Daily, Saren watched his actions to learn his preparations and fears. Saren feared for her father's wellbeing then, though silently. Soon, she would have only her memories of him to comfort her. His lessons and labors of yesterday would be her solace. She would remember his command and her promise.

CHAPTER TEN

The Royal Church

After the taxes taken by the Crown, there was no money left in Charles's purse for the offertory come Sunday. He could feel the eyes of other parishioners penetrating his back. Though he kept his chin held high, his breathing was rapid and rushed.

Without money for the brass offertory plate, citizens were not welcome to Sunday mass. Charles knew this but defied expectation and attended Church without sufficient coin.

Saren and Nan grew accustomed to having their suppers without Father's company, for the work of the King's knights was ongoing. Aside from the long journeys deep into the isolated towns, Father often arrived home late. He had time only to eat and sleep. Seldom did he remain awake long enough to read with Saren, as he had in seasons past.

When he was near, Saren habitually kept close to her father's every step. To not be under his feet, she quietly kept herself behind him as he went to his appointments around their cozy village, meeting with fellow royal knights and keeping tax collection civil, as his royal duties required. Beyond the village, in the countryside where sheep graced the hillsides, he discreetly helped to spread the forbidden English Bibles.

Saren's small frame gave her the appearance of one younger than she indeed was. People often spoke to her as a child, believing her so young that they carried on their usual conversations without thinking she might be listening or understanding. Even her father was guilty of this. He, too, would rail against the Church and Crown taxes without so much as a question or gesture from the girl. She listened.

Had she been born a boy; Saren would have been preparing for training as a royal knight. Instead, she followed behind her father, listening and learning everything necessary to become a Lollard Knight.

Father began to leave earlier each morning for his meetings around the countryside. Though seldom invited to join him, Saren rose before dawn to prepare pottage for his morning meal. She wrapped the remaining pottage paste in cloth for his noon meal. Silently, she would slip out of the house behind him. Once he noticed her, he only smiled and went about his way. He did not fight her traveling along because she was small, an only child, and without a mother. Saren was habitually quiet, never wanting for much along the way. And she often proved helpful. As Charles grew less diligent about keeping watch while walking the county roads, Saren kept a good lookout as they traveled, and she alerted him whenever they were followed by bandits.

Their travels were extensive. Though filled with questions and ideas of her own, Saren seldom spoke. Her silence provoked a need in her father to tell her of his tribulations.

During their recent journey home, he explained, "The Crown is unlawful, Saren. The Crown and the Church are one and the same." Charles held his breath before he continued. "The Church rules us, takes our monies and properties for unlawful taxes, tithing, and rents. Our King and his court are paid to keep silent and let the Church dictate their false truth." He stopped again to look at his young daughter.

With a sigh of what Saren later would recognize as frustration, Charles said, "The Royal Church forces the Crown to make rules and laws to fit their fellowship, not the word of God. The people are paying monies to be forgiven of sins that the Lord would forgive regardless of how much they could pay. The Church wants the people to continue to pay grandiose fees in exchange for heaven. Nowhere in the Bible does tithing ensure heaven. The people are being misled, and King Richard knows the truth, yet he has no control of his own Kingdom. The Holy Catholic Church does." The duo walked in silence while the moon continued its ascent. "Saren, we must be ever diligent about whom we trust. The times are uncertain if nothing more. I must trust Lord Percy—he is our friend." Charles quietly stroked his red beard, adding, "Though Percy is our constable, I do feel unease about his agenda."

Having heard her father speak of such matters during the weeks she followed him, Saren wished he had discussed more of what they had learned upon the Al-Aoura. "The Sophia of

Christ was most inspiring, Father. As we all are searches for the underlying reality of the universe and the plan, Jesus explains that whoever is worthy of knowledge will receive knowledge."

No more was said for the remainder of their walk home until the glow of a lantern silhouetted a prominent- cloaked figure before their brothy. "Keep close, child," Charles whispered.

Worry was fear manifest in Charles. He was not bestowed with courage. He tried to acquire bravery through these days of looming war, but all he could muster was carried in the weight of his weapon.

Cautiously, they approached their home.

The unexpected guest had entered the brothy before they arrived. Charles waved Saren to stand aside and peered through the door, hollering, "Hello, house." Then smiled and hastened Saren's approach. Charles recognized the old priest, Reverend Murphy, in his expansive brown cape wrapped tightly around his protruding belly. The low glow of the lantern's flame could not hide the stains and filth that adorned him nor the stench that permeated the room.

His voice and actions were snappy and bold, giving the man a cloak of arrogance as great as the size of his cape. This arrogance kept the reverend securely employed by the Crown. Charles knew that Reverend Murphy had arrived to bring him his next knightly assignment, as was often the routine.

The flame flickered and danced as Saren followed her father into their home. She closed the door behind her and placed her quiver of arrows upon the settle.

"Been hunting hare, my lass?" His dull eyes never looked directly into Saren's, but gazed around the room as he spoke. "Or 'er you and your pa scouting for bandits in the wood?" The dreary guest laughed heartily while holding his hand across his protruding belly. "Charles, your daughter here has been out hunting, has she not?" he announced with his empty chuckle.

However, Saren had yet to laugh.

"Reverend Murphy, we were on the road this day." Charles brushed the old priests' question aside.

"No merry men to come to call, dear lass?" the priest coaxed.

Saren, however, had lost her manners as her anger at the rude priest's contempt bubbled over. "I wouldn't marry for my life. I intend to cut my hair and wear trousers as soon as Father leaves, you see." Saren stood directly in front of the priest and said, "Reverend Murphy, I have yet to pay my respects this evening, my Dear Grace." She thrust her hand forward for him to kiss, for she was familiar with the father's ill regard for women. "I am Lady Saren Eadwine of Northumberland. I am a descendant of Eadwine, King of Deira. I am not looking for a husband or a family. Still, I devote my life and skills to perpetuating my father's works. Nor would I accept any proposal of marriage, were it to beckon. If you or any other has rebuke of this matter, I suggest you take your grievance to the King himself."

"There now, girl. Do as you will. There may be a dispute for the Crown. Your father may know that already." Reverend Murphy stepped toward Saren and took her small hand, raising it to his lips for a clammy kiss before turning away. Smiling, he added, "You have a fiery girl, Charles. Her timing is impeccable— the Earl of Northumberland, Lord Percy, has sent for your company." The plump priest's smile could cause suspicion among even the cruelest bandits. "Aye, lass, and Sir Charles, I have also brought a suitor's request from Sir Percy and his son Henry for Saren's presence at Alnwick Castle." The reverend's grin grew. "We have company approaching by way of the road: horses and men in full regalia collecting here near dawn to prepare to escort King Richard across the Irish Sea," he cackled. "Oh, the timing is delightful." Father Murphy looked past Saren. "Sir Percy swears this to be the new way of things. The only way, Sir Charles, is that Lord Percy has sent his order for your company at once. You will be accompanying King Richard across the Irish Sea." The reverend's lips shone with saliva, mirroring the fire's reflection.

"Why didn't you speak sooner, Reverend Murphy? What are we waiting for?" Charles hurried to gather a cloak, ignoring the omnipresent greed and malevolence permeating the priest's aura.

"Father, how dare you? We have already spoken of this. After all, we have discussed, I can't believe you would agree to something like this." Saren choked back the frustration that welled in her throat.

"Saren, lass, you know I would not do this behind your back."

Charles looked away from her eyes. "Wouldn't you consider it, though?" he pleaded.

Saren held her breath. She wished she could accompany them, but she refrained after her outburst toward Reverend Murphy. "Father, I choose to remain here, for if I go with you. You will be protecting my person, not your solemn duty." She ignored the request to meet the earl's son and silently prayed that it would be forgotten.

Charles cupped her tiny face, "Dear girl, you are much wiser than your years." Her father wiped a lone tear from her cheek. "And you know for certain that I knew nothing of this request from Lord Percy and his son, Sir Henry?"

She nodded. He smiled and mirrored her nod. "Good, now, my child. Please consider the possibility. It would bring me comfort while I'm away from you."

The priest walked outside, leaving the door ajar behind him for Charles to follow.

"I'd best make haste, my lass. I shan't be but a moment to learn my solemn duties." Charles removed Saren's grip from inside his vest, failing to notice the witnessing eyes of the priest beyond the door; he embraced her hands. "I shall tell all that I can soon, my girl." Reluctant to let go of her, he strode from the house toward Alnwick Castle to learn of his assignments.

Charles followed Friar Murphy, careful to stay ten steps behind him. Any other man of God, he would have walked at his side. Murphy, however, was not a man that Charles was pleased to accompany. And now that he had been disrespectful to his daughter while a guest under his roof, Charles had no obligation to treat him graciously and walked on keeping his stride in check.

CHAPTER ELEVEN

Preserving the Meat

"Nan," Saren ceased her singing in wonder. "Why does Father sing only songs of battle and war? Why doesn't he play the old hymns?"

Nan packed the stones higher around their growing coals to divert the encroaching tide. "Child, your father lost your mother and your many brothers. His only love that remains is his love for you. He is devoted to keeping you safe from harm." The aged woman looked to Saren and then out to sea, her blue eyes twinkling. "He is not of the Pagan realm as I am. As we are, child," Nan corrected herself. "He is only close to Mother Earth and her love when he plays music. Only then can your father find a type of peace in his heart. But now he has turned that music to battle hymns and rage." Nan looked at her strips of herring that marinated in their fire's smoke to preserve summer's bounty for winter reserves.

"Saren, your father imagines that he can return peace through his English Bibles?" she asked as much as she told.

"King Richard is ill-prepared and greedy. Though, he does support the endeavors to grant the people the freedom to hear their Lord's gospel in their native words."

Nan began her prayer to Mother Earth again. "Again, when you will send forth thy joyous day an' give nourishment of life with your eternal surety; and when the soul departs to you, we return." [18]

The day's work of preserving meats over the embers was nearly complete. The two women moved their bodies strikingly familiar as their prayer continued in song: "From thee, Father, and through The Mother, the two immortal names, Parents of thy divine being." [19]

"Nan, I shall help my father spread the Bible's words. I have heard them all my life and learned to read them."

"I know, Saren, my child. You will help him, an' you must." Nan sighed. "You have much to learn an' much more to share." She added, "Remember, my dear child. You are not alone in your endeavors. You always have me, your grandmamma, to help you." Nan stood from the burning coals upon the pebbled shore, squared herself directly facing Saren, and embraced her in her loving hug, patting her behind as she had since Saren's youth.

The Lord of Northumberland summoned Charles the week before his dreaded departure. Charles had prepared Saren for this peaceful Ireland expedition. Saren and her

Nan had packed rabbit, roots, and mushrooms smoked with dried herbs for his journey. His sword he sharpened as it glistened in the glow of flames of their meager cooking fire and the last remaining candle. Each man could bring one extra pair of woolen stockings and tunic and one doublet to be worn beneath the protective hauberk. Charles's helmet, also of boiled leather, was inferior to his rank among his comrades', yet he preferred it to the heavy chainmail version the other knights wore.

Lost in the mission to spread English Bibles across the land, Charles had forgotten his divine purpose of protecting the secret book entrusted to him. Protection of those secrets was now given to his daughter, and one small collection of arrows.

"The night is spent, Father. I shall wake to bid you farewell." Saren stood over her father as he wiped a leather cloth along the bone bow. She rested her open palm upon his shoulder, feeling his breathing beneath his woven tunic.

"Good night, lass." Charles looked up to his daughter. "Whit's fur ye'll no go past ye. I promise to wake ye early."

Charles prepared to leave before dawn; the sun lingered, caressing the horizon as he and Saren said farewell. "You 'er a strong girl, a lady now. I shall return before you realize 'at I have been away." Charles held on to his daughter like the tide's ebb-and-flow had ceased.

Her ebony curls draped across her shoulder, drawing her father to comb his fingers through them. The comfortable silence left room for the necessary conversation they both yearned to share.

"Saren, I knew of nothing of the contents of the book that I've given you until our visit to Barwick," Charles deeply inhaled. "The red seals, though open now, ought to be delivered to Jon the Mute at London's city center; he will take them to St. Othy's Priory, where Father Sautrey resides." He lifted a curl and dropped it to bounce upon her back. "And only if you feel threatened. We've held this book safe my entire life through. As my father before me and so on." Charles shut his eyes as he spoke. "The only knowledge I have is that the book was a gift from the Irish princess Darlugdach to King Eadwine's grandfather many centuries ago." Charles told all he could tell as rapidly as his mouth would allow. "I'm leaving, and I mustn't take them with me, girl. Ye are the only family left and the only one who can be trusted to keep them safe while I'm away." Charles shrugged his shoulders. "If ye must be rid of them, deliver them to London." Charles cradled Saren's small chin in his hand.

"You can do this knightly task, Saren. Be their protector and guardian while I am away, for none other than Father Sautrey knows of their existence. If I remain away after the other knights have returned home from Ireland, deliver them to Father Sautrey at St. Othy's Cathedral in London."

Charles stopped speaking. Dropping his shoulders with a sigh, he added, "Knowledge is power, my lass. An' all of man seeks power," he explained.

Saren wiped her tears on her father's shirt and smiled up at him, not yet ready to let him say his final farewell. She stood and felt again the comfort of their shared silence.

The dirt floor of their home left a musky smell in the room that Saren had grown indifferent to. Though, now, the earthy stench overwhelmed her. She blew out the candle's flame and sat silently as her father gathered his gear. They both were prepared for this, his departure.

Saren asked, "Father, I want to ask you to clarify for me and my troubles: does The Gospel of Mary reveal the underlying reality of the universe?"

"Bonnie Girl!" I don't know. I recollect that is what the disciples searched for, No? Is not that what we are all seeking? The plan of the universe. Is not that which we all seek? And did not Jesus himself explain that their speculations have not reached the truth?[3] I recall Joseph's interpretation he read upon the Al-Aoura that Providence has no wisdom in it. And fate does not discern. But to you it is given to know; and whoever is worthy of knowledge will receive it."[20]

Charles watched her return to the settle. It was a moment when words would not suffice. He sat near his daughter, brushing her shoulder slightly to soothe his emotions about his encroaching departure.

Without words to comfort or soothe, Charles lifted his pipes to his lips and played a melody of life for her spirit's sake. Rich were his notes. Deep in his heart, he played with his love for her. Longer than he ought to have lingered, Charles remained and played. The candles' smoke subsided, and the wax no longer dripped, yet he played on. There came a rapping at their door. Charles rose to go and swung his pipes across his shoulder. Bending to Saren's ear, he whispered, "You are well prepared. And are never alone."

Saren pressed his hand tight upon her shoulder, looking up into his eyes, saying, "I am love, I am wise, and I promise to keep the secret book safe."

A note from the author

I invite you to join our voices in conversation and in a song about the Morningstar series: Saren's journey of divination as a body and soul in Man's world, listening to the voice of love within. The God within.

Please join Morningstar's group here:

https://www.facebook.com/groups/booksforgirls

About The Author

*O*ndi Laure is a 5th generation native to the wilds of Wyoming. She is best known for her tales of humanity's savage past. She writes of untold history, wisdom, and courage of those who protected repressed sacred feminine qualities of the universe in her novel, Morningstar. For over a decade, Ondi has helped others achieve alignment with their story's purpose and to identify as an author in her Aligned Writing program. She has been featured in Forbes and Top Talent magazines. Her clients include Susan and Jacob Browder, Callie Katz, and Farzana Ebrahimi, and she has shared the stage with Isabel Dondadeo, Kathi Tait, Allison Lewis, and Kedra Davies. She has done everything from writing and publishing books to mountaineering and backcountry guiding across the Continental Divide. When she isn't writing and skiing with family or friends, she plays her guitar or trains horses with her husband, Matt.

To learn more about the author and Book Two, The Forbidden Bibles, visit: https://ondilaure.com

Cited Sources

2, Bible Manuscript Society, 1382 Wycliffe Bible;
https://biblemanuscriptsociety.com/Bible-resources/
English-Bible-History/Wycliffe-Bible

8 Coogan, M. A Brief Introduction to the Old Testament:
The Hebrew Bible in its Context. (Oxford University Press:
Oxford 2009). p. 369; (Psalm 78:14)

18-20 https://greywolf.druidry.co.uk/2013/04/12th-century-
english-prayer-tomother- earth

6-7, 10 Grey Wolf. A Prayer to Mother Earth: 12th Century.
https://greywolf.druidry.co.uk/2013/04/12th-century-
english-prayer-to-mother-earth/

2–5 Luminarium. *Anthology of English Literature*, "The Ballad of Chevy Chase." http://www.luminarium.org/medlit/
medlyric/chevychase.htm

9, 14 Pagels, "What Became of God the Mother?" in Wom-
anspirit Rising. Carol P. Christ and Judith Plaskow (Harper
& Row, 1979), 109.

1 The Gospel According to Mary Magdalene (The Gospel of Mary) http://www.gnosis.org/library/marygosp.htm

11, 13Stephan Patterson & Marvin Meyer. The Gnostic Society Library, The Nag Hammadi Library. *The Gospel of Thomas.* http://gnosis.org/naghamm/gosthom.html

12, Textus Receptus. *John Wycliffe Bible 1382*, Proverbs 8:22-23, 27,30. http://textusreceptusbibles.com/

2, Wycliffe Associates and Simons, Keith. Easy English Bibles: 2005. https://www.easyenglish.bible/ The Sophia of Jesus Christ hppt://www.earlychirstianwritings.com/text/Sophia.html